I am feeling...

More words for my feelings:

Furious   Defensive   Resentful

I am feeling...

Happy

Hopeful ### Pleased

More words for my feelings:

Optimistic   Inspired   Delighted

I am feeling...

Scared

Nervous

Afraid

More words for my feelings:

Overwhelmed   Terrified   Shocked

I am feeling...

- Excited
- Interested
- Cheerful

More words for my feelings:

Energetic　　　Eager　　　Entertained

I am feeling...

Tired

Bored

Lazy

More words for my feelings:

Unmotivated   Indifferent   Drained

I am feeling...

Silly

Playful   Funny

More words for my feelings:

Giggly   Unfocused   Scatty

I am feeling...

Annoyed

Jealous

Frustrated

More words for my feelings:

Defensive   Agitated   Irritated

I am feeling...

Amazing

Fantastic　　　　　　　　　　Brilliant

More words for my feelings:

Creative　　　　　　Passionate　　　　　　Inspired

I am feeling...

Worried

Nervous   Confused

More words for my feelings:

Anxious   Uncomfortable   Indecisive

I am feeling...

Loving

Caring

Kind

More words for my feelings:

Grateful   Affectionate   Appreciative

I am feeling...

Sad

Lonely

Low

More words for my feelings:

Insecure   Disappointed   Rejected

I am feeling...

- Ready
- Focused
- Brave

More words for my feelings:

Motivated   Confident   Daring

I am feeling...

- Upset
- Hurt
- Hopeless

More words for my feelings:

Miserable   Devastated   Rejected

I am feeling...

Calm

Safe

Relaxed

More words for my feelings:

Comfortable   Satisfied   Peaceful

Keep the conversations going with a feelings wheel poster visit www.mywellbeingschool.com for more inspiring resources

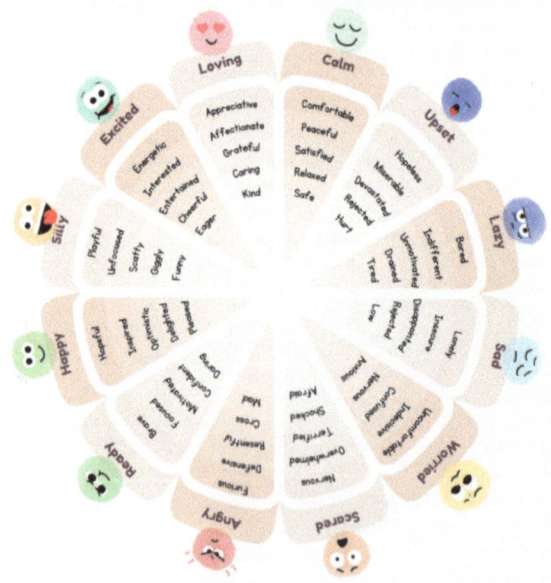

More books on feelings and emotions by H. J. Ray

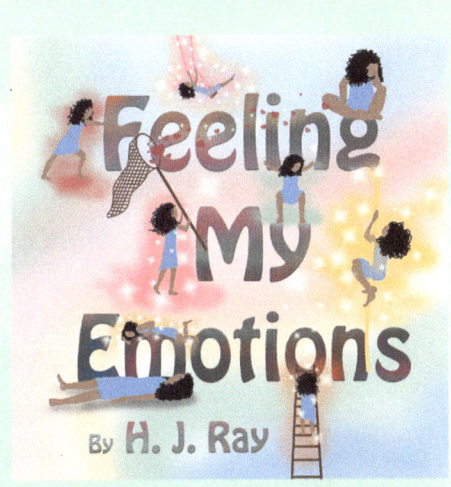

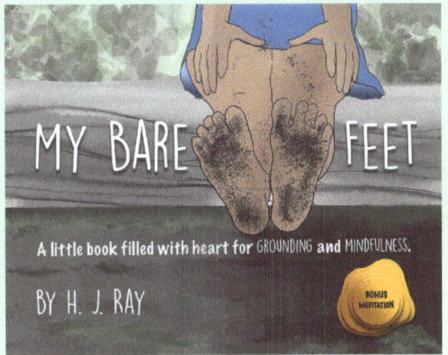

Hi, my name is Heather Ray,

I'm a neurodivergent author/illustrator & founder of My Wellbeing School. I'm on a mission to spread joy, light, and creativity.

If you loved this book, please consider leaving a review. Your support means the world!

Thank you.

www.mywellbeingschool.com

www.ingramcontent.com/pod-product-compliance
Lightning Source LLC
Chambersburg PA
CBHW041203290426
44109CB00003B/113